This

TW  **HOOTS**

book belongs to

. . . .

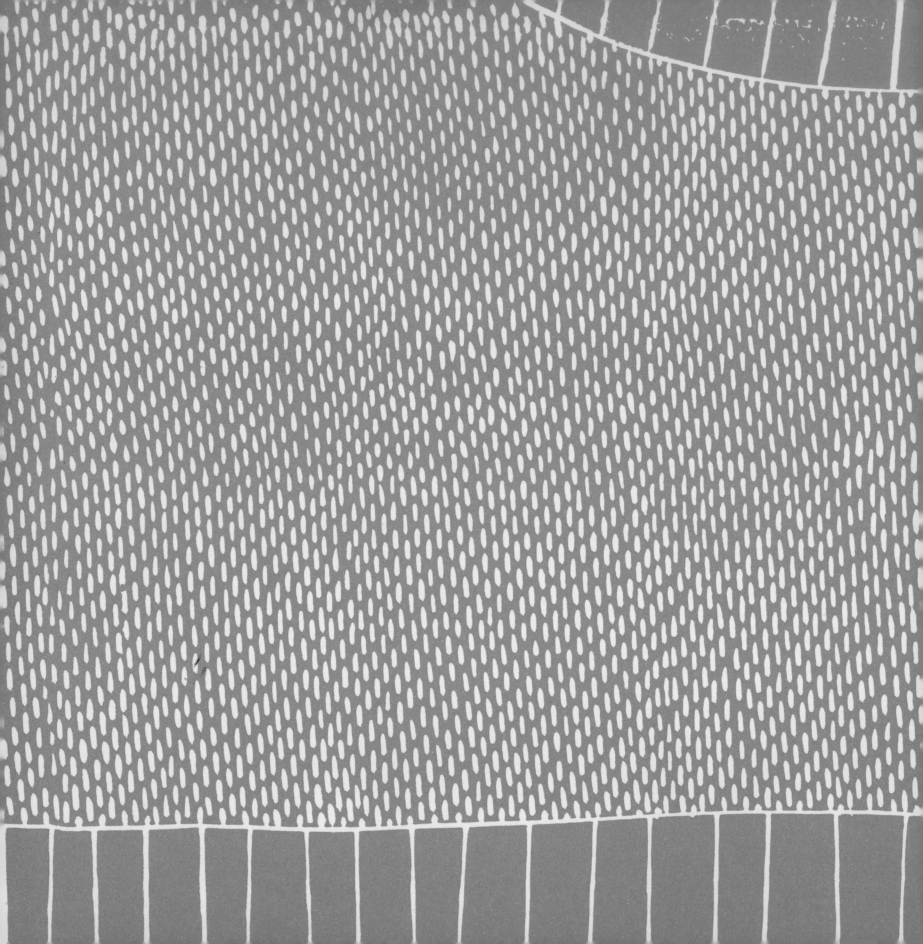

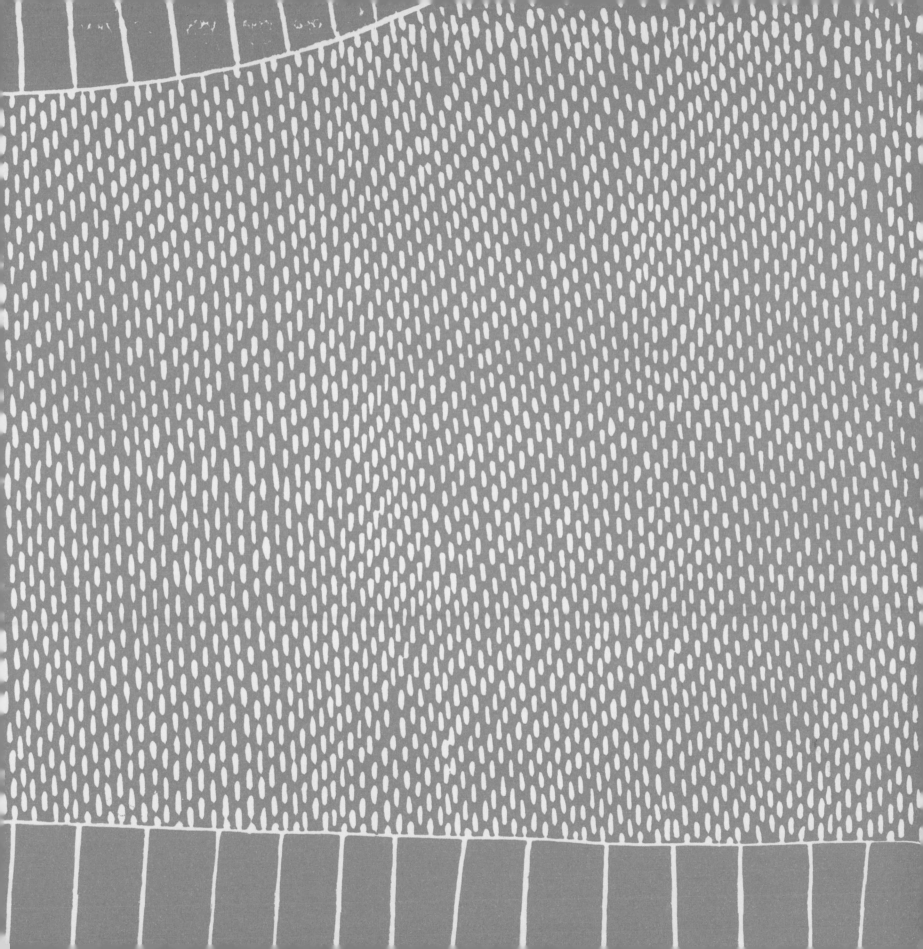

FOR MY NEPHEW YLFINGUR

First published 2019 by Two Hoots

This edition published 2020 by Two Hoots

an imprint of Pan Macmillan

The Smithson, 6 Briset Street, London EC1M 5NR

Associated companies throughout the world

www.panmacmillan.com

ISBN 978-1-5098-4297-1

Text and illustrations copyright © Morag Hood 2019, 2020

Moral rights asserted.

A CIP catalogue record for this book is available from the British Library.

Printed in China

The illustrations in this book were created using lino print and collage.

www.twohootsbooks.com

MORAG HOOD

BRENDA IS A SHEEP

TW🦉 HOOTS

These are sheep.

This is also a sheep.

This sheep is called Brenda.

Brenda has a very nice woolly jumper.

Brenda does all the things that sheep do . . .

... because Brenda is a sheep.

The sheep learn lots of new games
from their friend Brenda.

Like catch,

teeth sharpening,

and tag. Brenda loves tag.

But no matter how hard she tries ...

... she can never catch anyone.
They always get away.

The sheep think Brenda is probably the best sheep they have ever met.

She is so very tall, has nice pointy teeth,
and her wool is all knitted and colourful.

All the sheep want to be just like Brenda.

But Brenda
has other things
on her mind.

She is working
hard on her special
mint sauce recipe.

The sheep have never had Brenda's special
mint sauce but she tells them it is very tasty.

You just need to find the right thing
to eat it with.

Luckily, Brenda knows just the thing. She is getting ready for a feast.

The sheep are very excited.

Brenda tells the sheep to go to bed nice and early. She says there will be a surprise for them in the morning.

A delicious surprise.

Brenda has to wait a very long
time for the sheep to go to sleep.

But at last they begin to nod off, one by one.
Brenda counts them on her claws.

One yummy sheep,

two yummy sheep,

three yummy sheep . . .

ZZZZZZZZZ

By the time Brenda wakes up, the sheep
have made a surprise of their own.

There is
grass stew

and grass
pie

and grass
burgers

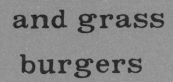

and grass
lasagne

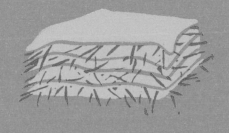

and grass
sandwiches

and grass
sausages.

And for pudding,
grass biscuits.

With a delicious
sauce to pour
over it all.

This is not the feast Brenda had planned.

But when she sees everything
her friends have done for her,

Brenda can't help but
join in the fun.
Because, after all . . .

Brenda is a sheep.

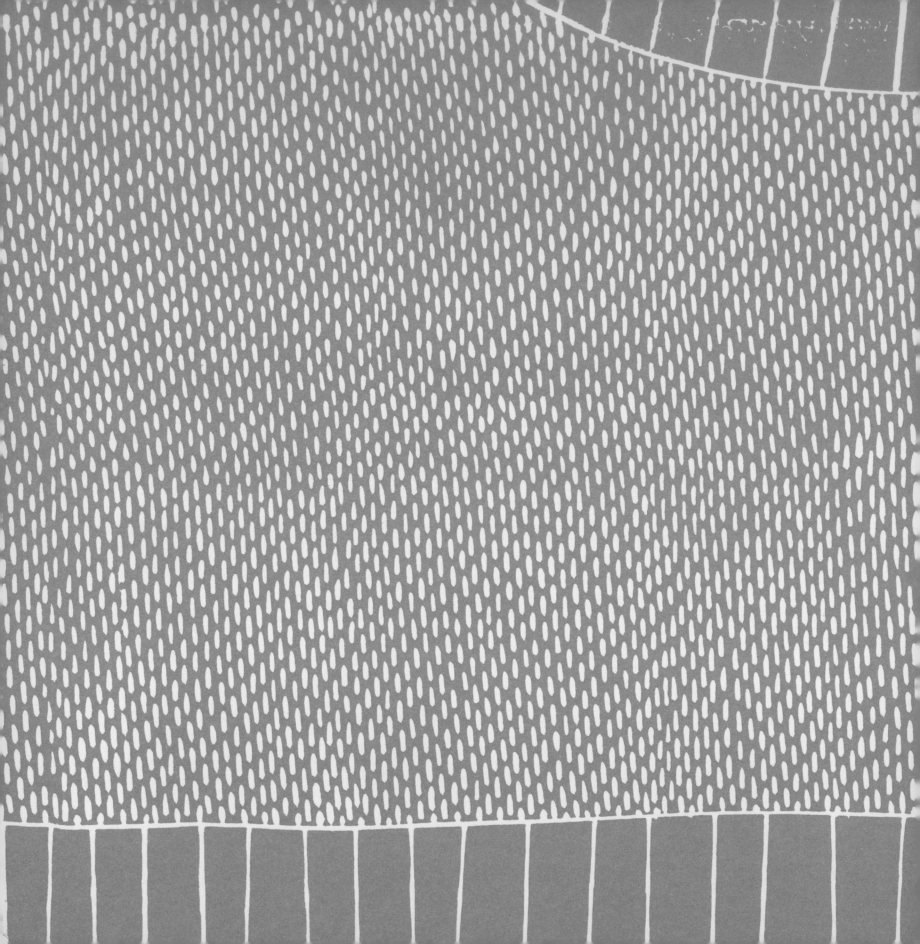

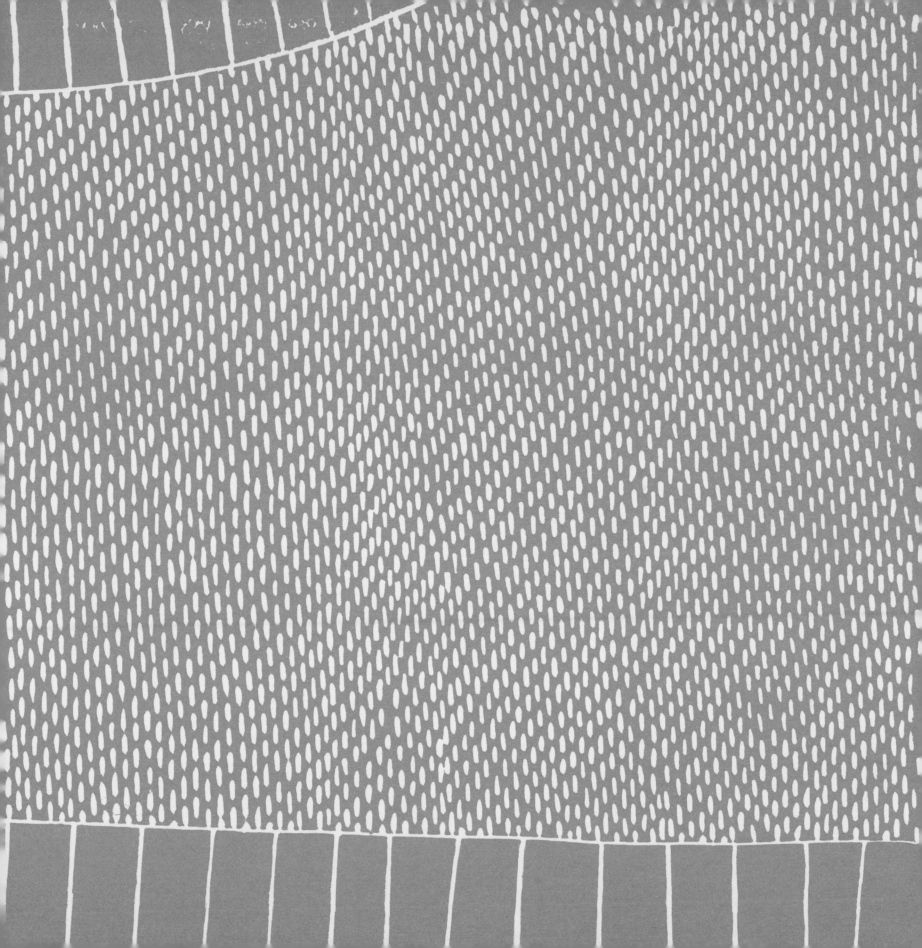

HOW TO DRAW SHEEP

Start with some fluffy clouds (or a nice woolly jumper).

Add four legs (and maybe a tail).

Give them each a head.

SHEEP!